AMANDA PIG, SCHOOLGIRL

Jean Van Leeuwen

PICTURES BY

ANN SCHWENINGER

DIAL BOOKS FOR YOUNG READERS
NEW YORK

For Elizabeth, schoolgirl
J.V.L.

For Judy Lanfredi
A.S.

Published by
Dial Books for Young Readers
A Member of Penguin Putnam Inc.
375 Hudson Street
New York, New York 10014

Printed in Hong Kong
The Dial Easy-to-Read logo is a registered trademark of
Dial Books for Young Readers,
a division of Penguin Books USA Inc., ® TM 1,162,718.

Library of Congress Cataloging in Publication Data
Van Leeuwen, Jean.
Amanda Pig, schoolgirl/by Jean Van Leeuwen;
pictures by Ann Schweninger.—1st ed.
p. cm.
Summary: Amanda Pig's first day of school is every
bit as wonderful as she always hoped it would be.
ISBN 0-8037-1980-9 (trade)
ISBN 0-8037-1981-7 (lib.)
[1. First day of school—Fiction.
2. Schools—Fiction. 3. Pigs—Fiction.]
I. Schweninger, Ann, ill. II. Title.
PZ7.V3273Ap 1997 [Fic]—dc20 95-53062 CIP AC

First Edition
5 7 9 10 8 6 4

The full-color artwork was prepared using carbon pencil,
colored pencils, and watercolor washes. It was then scanner-separated
and reproduced as red, blue, yellow, and black halftones.

Reading Level 1.9

CONTENTS

LOLLIPOP

Finally, finally, finally

it was the day Amanda had waited for.

She hopped out of bed.

She put on her new purple party dress

and her new pink hair ribbons.

"There," said Amanda. "I'm all ready."

She went to find Mother.

"Is it time?" she asked.

Mother opened her eyes.

"Even the sun is not up yet," she said.

"You will have to wait a little longer."

"I have been waiting my whole life,"
said Amanda, "to go to school."

She played school with her animals

until the sun came up.

"Now is it time?"

she asked at breakfast.

"Not quite," said Father.

Amanda said good-bye to Sallie Rabbit.

"Too bad you're too little for school,"

she said. "But don't worry.

I will play with you when I get home."

She tucked Sallie in for a nap.

"Now?" she asked.

"Now!" said Oliver.

At the bus stop

Mother and Father hugged Amanda.

"Have fun, schoolgirl," said Father.

"I will!" said Amanda.

She hopped up the high bus steps

and found a seat with Oliver.

Oliver knew everyone on the bus.

"Hello, Bernard!" he called.

"Hi, Rosie. Hi, Alexander."

Soon he was talking and laughing

with his friends.

Amanda didn't know anyone. Not yet.

In the next seat was someone her size.

"Hello," said Amanda.

The someone did not answer.

She was sucking on a red lollipop.

"I like lollipops," said Amanda.

"Purple is my best flavor."

The someone did not answer.

"My name is Amanda," said Amanda.

"This is my first day of school

and I have a new dress."

The someone still did not answer.

She looked as if she were going to cry.

"Are you scared?" asked Amanda.

The someone nodded her head.

"I'm not," said Amanda. "School is fun.

You will like it. You'll see."

The bus stopped

and everyone started to get off.

"I will take you to your room,"

said Oliver.

Amanda took the someone's hand.

"Come on," she said.

Together they followed Oliver

down the high bus steps and

through the wide halls to their room.

"Good-bye," said Oliver.

"Hello," said the teacher.

"I am Mrs. Flora Pig."

"I am Amanda," said Amanda.

"And who is this?" asked the teacher.

The someone did not answer.

"This," said Amanda, "is Lollipop."

THE CIRCLE

In Mrs. Flora Pig's room

there was so much to do,

Amanda didn't know what to do first.

She played in the dress-up corner.

"Look, Lollipop," she said.

"I'm a farmer astronaut."

She played in the make-believe corner.

"I can't believe it," she said.

"A whole suitcase full of puppets.

Hi, Mr. Rabbit. You should meet

my rabbit. Her name is Sallie."

She played in the building corner.

"I never saw so many blocks," she said.

"I'll make a skyscraper. Or a city.

Or maybe the whole world!"

Mrs. Flora Pig's room had giant ABC's
and a piano and boxes called cubbies.

"Cubbies?" said Amanda.

"What are those for?"

"For things you bring to school
and the work you take home,"
said Mrs. Flora Pig.

"I want to do a lot of work,"
said Amanda.

"Soon we will," said Mrs. Flora Pig.
"But right now we are going to sit
in a circle and get to know each other."

Amanda saw a circle of little chairs

and one big one.

The big one must be for me,

she thought,

because I am so big now.

Amanda sat in the big chair.

Mrs. Flora Pig sat next to her.

But something was wrong.

Her knees were next to her ears.

"That's the teacher's chair, silly,"

said a tiny boy.

"Oops," said Amanda.

She and the teacher changed chairs.

"Now we are going to play a game,"
said Mrs. Flora Pig.

"I call it the name game."

She pointed at herself.

"My name is Mrs. Flora Pig," she said.

"And I like to play the piano."

She pointed at the tiny boy.

"My name is William," said the boy.

"And I like big trucks."

She pointed at a girl dressed in pink.

"My name is Lily," said the girl.

"And I like my baby sister."

She pointed at Lollipop.

Lollipop didn't say anything.

Instead of her lollipop,

she was sucking her thumb.

"Why doesn't she talk?" asked William.

"She will talk when she is ready,"

said Mrs. Flora Pig.

"Maybe today. Maybe tomorrow."

She pointed at Amanda.

"My name is Amanda," said Amanda.
"And I like ballet and my new dress
and Sallie Rabbit and ice cream
and my brother Oliver and purple
and singing songs.

But the very best thing I like

is being a schoolgirl."

"How nice," said Mrs. Flora Pig.

THE PLAYGROUND

Mrs. Flora Pig played the piano

and everyone sang.

Everyone except Lollipop.

Mrs. Flora Pig read a silly story

and everyone laughed.

Everyone except Lollipop.

Then it was time to go out

to the playground.

"Oh, good!" said Amanda.

"I love swings and slides

and monkey bars."

Everyone was swinging and sliding

and climbing and jumping.

Everyone except Lollipop.

"Come on, Lollipop," said Amanda.

"Let's have fun."

But Lollipop sat in the sandbox

with a sad face.

"Please don't be sad," said Amanda.

"I am your friend."

"Me too," said Lily.

"Me three," said William.

"I bet I can make Lollipop smile."

He walked up the slide,

slid down very fast,

and did a somersault at the bottom.

"Ta-dah!" he said.

Amanda laughed.

But Lollipop did not smile.

"Look at me," said Lily.

She climbed high on the monkey bars,

hung upside down by her knees,

and made funny faces.

"How's that?" she asked.

But Lollipop did not smile.

"Watch this," said a boy named Sam.

He bounced a ball on his head. *Boing!*

And on his knees. *Boing!*

And on his nose. *Boing, boing!*

But Lollipop did not smile.

Amanda tried to think of a trick

she could do.

She wasn't very good at somersaults

or ball or hanging by her knees.

But she could dance.

"Look, Lollipop!" she said.

Amanda danced around the sandbox.

She twirled around the swings.

"And now for my pirouette," she said.

She spun around.

Faster and faster she went.

It was the most wonderful pirouette

she had ever done.

"Uh-oh," said Amanda.

Suddenly she felt dizzy.

The swings and slides and sandbox
all seemed to be spinning.
So were Lily and Sam and Sam's ball.

"Help!" cried Amanda.
The ball bounced on her head
and she fell into the sandbox.

Amanda opened her eyes.

There was Lollipop looking at her.

And she was smiling.

"She did it!" cried Amanda, jumping up.

"Lollipop smiled!"

And Lollipop smiled again.

PICTURES

"Our room is just perfect,"

said Mrs. Flora Pig.

"Except for one thing."

Amanda looked around.

"The walls are so plain," she said.

"They look lonely," said Lily.

"Exactly," said Mrs. Flora Pig.

"If only I had some nice pictures.

Pictures of you."

"We could make you some," said Amanda.

"Really big ones," said William.

"Good idea," said Mrs. Flora Pig.

She took out a long roll of paper.

"Lie down, please," she said.

She traced all around William.

Then she cut out a William shape.

"Now I have a life-size William

for my wall," she said.

"Do me!" said Amanda.

"And me!" said Sam.

Mrs. Flora Pig did everyone.

Then she put out scissors and glue

and crayons and buttons and beads

and bits of ribbon and lace

and all sorts of things.

"Now you can decorate

your pictures of you," she said.

Amanda worked hard on her picture.

First she colored her dress.

She used up a whole purple crayon.

Then she saw the lace. "Oh!" she said.

"I can make a ballet costume."

She glued lace all over everything

and made ribbons for her hair.

Finally she drew the biggest smile

in all the world.

"I'm finished," she said.

"How nice to have a happy Amanda
for my wall," said Mrs. Flora Pig.

She hung Amanda on the wall
next to William.

Soon everyone was on the wall.

Everyone except Lollipop.

"Wow!" said Amanda. "Lollipop
is coloring a hundred flowers."

"Look," said Sam.
"She even made a lollipop
out of a button and a Popsicle stick."
Lollipop smiled.
She colored her last flower.

"What a beautiful dress,"
said Mrs. Flora Pig.
She hung Lollipop on the wall
next to Amanda.

"Now my wall isn't lonely anymore,"
she said. "I have Lily and Sam
and William and Amanda and . . ."

Suddenly Lollipop was whispering

in Amanda's ear.

"Emily!" said Amanda.

"She told me her name. It's Emily."

Mrs. Flora Pig smiled.

"Welcome, Emily," she said.

They all cleaned up.

Then it was time to go home.

"Come on, Lollipop,

I mean Emily," said Amanda.

"We can sit together on the bus."

Emily whispered in her ear again.

"Okay," said Amanda.

"I will call you Lollipop."

Amanda took Lollipop's hand.

And together the two schoolgirls

walked through the wide halls

and up the high steps onto the bus.